Bleau Discovers Pearl's Wisdom

Jesus Loves You

♡ Allyson K Horton

Bleau Discovers Pearl's Wisdom

The Adventures of a Golden Retriever and a Border Collie

Allyson Kelly Horton

Xulon Press
2301 Lucien Way #415
Maitland, FL 32751
407.339.4217
www.xulonpress.com

Illustrated by Michaela Keller

Unless otherwise indicated, Scripture quotations taken from the Holy Bible, New International Version (NIV). Copyright © 1973, 1978, 1984, 2011 by Biblica, Inc.™. Used by permission. All rights reserved.

Printed in the United States of America.

Paperback ISBN-13: 978-1-66283-567-4
Hardcover ISBN-13: 978-1-66283-568-1
Ebook ISBN-13: 978-1-66283-569-8

To all the children that God has allowed to be a part of the ministry that He has called me to and who have listened to all my stories…you will always and forever be "Allo's Kids." Always remember, "You may be sure your sins will find you out." Numbers 32:23

To my mother, Edwina, who always believes the best in me and pushes me to continue the pursuit of God's calling on my life, I finally kept my promise to "write a book one day." I love you.

To Dr. Wendy King, who gives such great care and love to Pearl and especially Bleau and all his mishaps as a regular visitor to see the vet…thank you for your compassion and love for all the pets that come into your care.

"However, I consider my life worth nothing to me, my only aim is to finish the race and complete the task the Lord Jesus has given me—the task of testifying to the Good News of God's grace" (Acts 20:24).

Pearl, the Border Collie, came to live with Wendy first. She loved her new home because there was so much room to run and explore outside. She was very wise, and her favorite thing to do was to chase the butterflies. When people came to visit, she would smile by showing her teeth, but sometimes people thought that she was growling at them. It didn't take long for them to find out she was being friendly—if not by her smile, then by her wagging tail.

Bleau was a Golden Retriever that was a gift to Wendy from her friend Mary. He got his name because he had blue eyes. What a precious, snuggly puppy he was! Bleau loved to chew everything when he was a puppy—the books Wendy was trying to read, the house plants Wendy was growing, and even the remote control to the television! He had always been mischievous, but Bleau was also very playful. He loved to chase birds, retrieve his bouncy ball, and splash and swim in his blue swimming pool.

Pearl and Bleau had many adventures together, and Pearl always helped Bleau to learn important lessons about life.

SAFE

Bleau loved to play ball.

Bleau loved to swim.

Bleau loved to take walks!

Bleau wanted to run free and explore.

Bleau did NOT like to wear a leash!

Because his Master Wendy loved him, she put him on a leash to go for a walk. This was not to keep him from having fun. It was not to keep him from being free, and it was not to keep him from exploring. The leash was to keep Bleau SAFE…

So he wouldn't get hit by a car...

So he wouldn't get lost...

So a stranger didn't take him away...

When Bleau walked on his leash, Wendy kept him safe! He still got to enjoy his walk and all the fun things to explore.

Pearl's Wisdom

God gave us rules to follow in the Bible. The rules were not made to keep us from having fun or keep us from exploring this great big world…the rules God gave us were to keep us safe and to keep us close to Him! In Exodus 20, God gave us ten rules to follow that would allow us to have peace with God and with each other.

1. Love God more than anything else.
2. Don't make anything more important than God.
3. Always say God's name with love and respect.
4. Honor the Lord by resting on the seventh day of the week.
5. Love and respect your mom and dad.
6. Never hurt anyone.
7. Always be faithful to your husband or wife.
8. Don't take anything that isn't yours.
9. Always tell the truth.
10. Be happy with what you have. Don't wish for other people's things.

Later, in the New Testament, Jesus told us that just two rules could help us do all ten of these rules. He said, "Thou shalt love the Lord your God with all your heart, with all your soul, with all your strength and with all your mind; and you must love your neighbor as yourself" (Luke 10:27 NIV).

Lost

When the door opened, Pearl bolted through, and Bleau followed his big sister running fast to the forest.

Pearl ran fast, and so did Bleau. They went deep into the woods, so far you could barely see the sun.

Pearl and Bleau stopped fast when they heard a howling from the shadows behind the trees.

A coyote jumped out and grabbed Bleau by the tail and tumbled him to the ground. Round and round they went as Pearl ran as fast as she could back home.

Finally, Bleau was able to run and hide, curling up under a log as it began to get dark. He was hurt, he was scared, and he was sad. He wondered where Pearl was and thought he would never get home again.

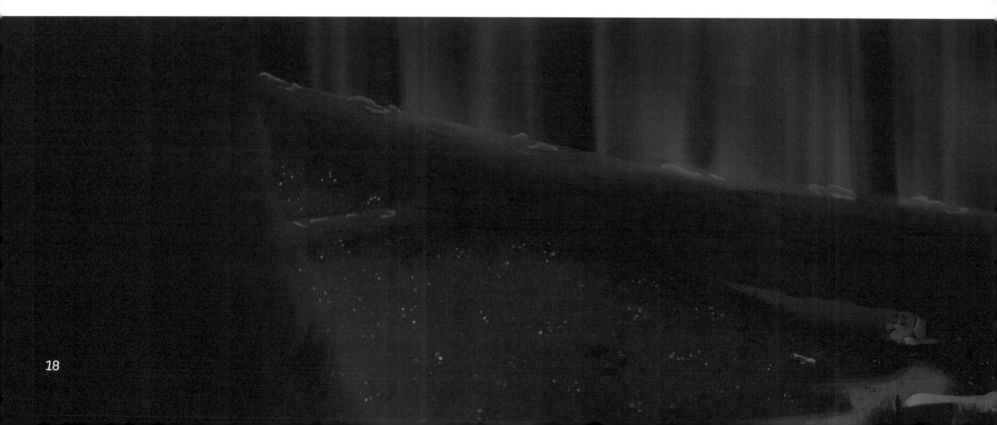

Back at home, a search was underway. Wendy and her friends went up and down the road, calling out "Bleau! Bleau!" But Bleau was too afraid to come out.

When it was dark and Wendy and her friends could no longer see, the search had to end. Bleau, still hiding under the log, was sad. He was hungry. He was scared. He wanted to be with Wendy and Pearl.

Wendy and Pearl missed Bleau that night, so they left a light on and a bowl of water on the porch just in case Bleau found his way home. It was a long, long night for Bleau.

The next morning, Wendy and her friend Ryan followed a trail into the forest, shouting, "Bleau! Bleau!" Bleau lifted his ears—he thought he heard his name! The sun was shining bright, and he wasn't so sad anymore. But he was very hungry, and he wanted to go home. He stood up and limped toward the sound of his name.

Bleau reached a path and put his nose to the ground, following the scent down the path.

Just when the woods ended and the sun brightened, he looked up and saw the best thing he had ever seen. He ran as fast as his tired, dirty, hungry, and hurt self could go.

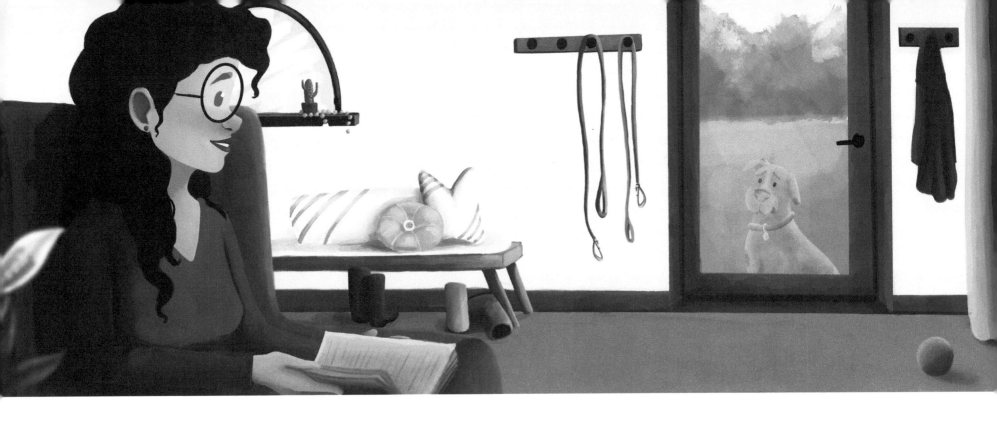

He ran up the steps and stood in front of the glass door of his house and looked in. Wendy looked up and saw him standing there.

With a shout and a yell, Wendy opened the door and welcomed Bleau home.

Bleau was finally in the arms of the one who loved him most. His tail was wagging as he was fed, given water to drink, given a bath, and had his wounds from the coyote bandaged. Bleau crawled next to Wendy, exhausted, and fell soundly asleep. He was not afraid anymore. He was not hungry anymore. He was safe. He was home. He was happy.

Pearl's Wisdom

Have you ever been lost? Were you scared? Have you ever lost something that was very valuable to you? In the Bible, there is a story about some things that were lost (Luke 15) …

A sheep,

A coin,

A son!

In this story, everything that was lost was found! Jesus wants us to know that He wants us to be found by Him! He tells us in Luke 10:10 that He came to seek and to save the lost!

Fear

Every time the clouds got dark, and the wind began to blow, Bleau looked for a place to hide.

His favorite hiding places were under the porch where no one could see him, and if he was inside the house, he hid behind the couch.

When the storm came and the thunder boomed in the sky, Bleau began to tremble and shake because he was so afraid. Wendy would pet him, sing to him, and turn on some music to keep him from hearing the rumble of the thunder. Bleau didn't come out of hiding until the storm had passed by.

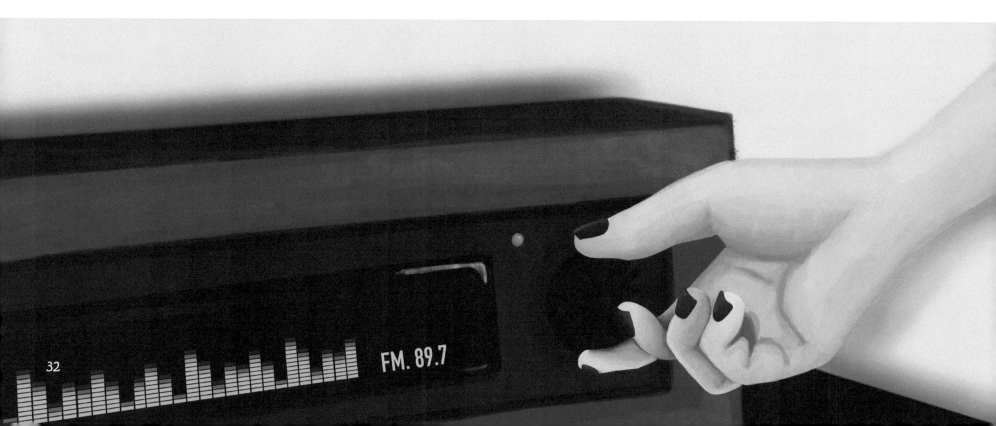

FM. 89.7

Finally, Bleau came out to play.

Pearl's Wisdom

What are you afraid of? Are you, like Bleau, afraid of thunderstorms? Are you afraid of the dark?

The Bible tells us 365 times, "Do not be afraid." That is one verse for each day of the year!

Any time you are afraid, you can ask God to help you.

Here are two of my favorite Bible verses about fear:

"Have I not commanded you? Be strong and courageous. Do not be afraid, for the Lord your God will be with you wherever you go" (Joshua 1:9 NIV).

"When I am afraid, I will put my trust in you" (Psalm 56:3 NIV).

What is your favorite Bible verse about fear? There are so many to choose from!

Wise Pearl has helped Bleau to learn some important lessons from all their adventures.

Wendy, Pearl, and Bleau want all the children to know that the Bible is a special book that tells you how very much God loves you, that you do not have to be afraid, and that even if you are lost, God is with you!

When you read the Bible, you will be wise to do what it says!

"Thy Word (the Bible) is a lamp unto my feet, and a light unto my path…" (Ps. 119:105).

"Be DOERS of the Word (the Bible) and not hearers only…" (James 1:22).

Allyson Kelly Horton is from Blythewood, South Carolina. She graduated in 1987 with a BA degree in Physical Education from Columbia College and then attended Southwestern Baptist Theological Seminary in Fort Worth, Texas, receiving a MA in Religious Education in 1991.

She began her ministry in 1991 in Sylacauga, Alabama. Since 2005, she has been the Children Minister at Spring Valley Baptist Church in Columbia, South Carolina.

Allyson's favorite thing about ministry is leading children to a relationship with Christ and watching her children grow in their faith. Although she has no kids of her own, she loves that she gets "paid to play" with the terrific kids at SVBC and take them on life-changing mission trips. Pearl and Bleau are often used as object lessons to help children understand the concepts of a spiritual lesson from the Bible, so during the down time in ministry because of the COVID-19 pandemic, she wrote those stories into her first children's book, *Bleau Discovers Pearls of Wisdom*.

For fun she likes to attend Clemson games and travel.

Michaela Keller is an artist from South Carolina. There are two constant things in Michaela's life—drawing and animals.

When Michaela was a young girl, you would either find her with a pencil or a frog in her hand. As she grew up, she decided that art was what she wanted to do for the rest of her life, so she went to Savannah College of Art and Design to become a 3D animator.

This is Michaela's first published illustration. She jumped at the offer to create a children's book because picture books were always her favorite growing up. Being able to combine her two passions of drawing and animals has been a dream come true!

CPSIA information can be obtained
at www.ICGtesting.com
Printed in the USA
BVHW050504310122
627163BV00001BA/2

9 7 8 1 6 6 2 8 3 5 6 8 1